HODDER CHILDREN'S BOOKS
First published in Great Britain in 2017 by Hodder and Stoughton

Text copyright © Peter Bently, 2017
Illustrations copyright © Garry Parsons, 2017

A CIP catalogue record for this book is available
from the British Library.

HB ISBN: 978 1 444 93389 5
PB ISBN: 978 1 444 93390 1

10 9 8 7 6 5 4 3 2 1

Printed and bound in China

MIX
Paper from
responsible sources
FSC
www.fsc.org
FSC® C104740

Hodder Children's Books
An imprint of Hachette Children's Group
Part of Hodder and Stoughton
Carmelite House
50 Victoria Embankment
London EC4Y 0DZ

An Hachette UK Company
www.hachette.co.uk
www.hachettechildrens.co.uk

For Connie and Sissy – P.B.

For Codie and Kyle – G.P.

Happy Easter, Tooth Fairy!

PETER BENTLY & GARRY PARSONS

Hodder Children's Books

The Tooth Fairy looked out one bright Easter day
and saw an old friend who was hopping her way.
She waved from the window. "Hello, Easter Bunny!
Do you fancy a nice hot cross bun with some honey?"

The bunny said, "Sorry, I really can't stay!
I'm off to hide eggs for the egg hunt today."

"I'll help!" said the fairy.
"That sounds like great fun!"
The bunny said, "Thanks!
We'll soon get it done."

The fairy flew over a fence with her eggs and the bunny slipped through on his lollopy legs.

The Tooth Fairy laughed,
"Hiding eggs is a hoot!"
as she dropped one –kerplop!–
in an old welly boot.

She hid eggs in a wheelbarrow,

under a log,

then got chased by a kitten

and Tim Tucker's dog!

Some gardens were massive and some very small.
The bunny and fairy hid eggs in them all.

"Just **one** garden left!"
said the bunny at last.
"The hunt will start soon
so we'll have to work fast."

They crept through the hedge
and dashed madly about
hiding their eggs –
till they heard someone shout.

The Tooth Fairy cried,
"Someone's coming! Oh my!"

So they stood still as gnomes
as three children ran by.

One girl, little Gracie, was ever so giggly.
"Look at my tooth," she declared. "It's all wiggly!"

Said the bunny, "We need to hide somewhere! But **where?**"

The Tooth Fairy pointed and said, "**Over there!** Let's hide in that watering can for a bit."

But the poor bunny's **ears** were too big to fit!

The Tooth Fairy helped him
to pull out his head.

POP!

Then he dived in a bin that stood next to the shed.

The egg hunt began and off Gracie ran –
straight for the Tooth Fairy's watering can!

"Is there something inside?"
Gracie said with a frown –
then she gleefully shook
the whole can upside down!

The fairy just managed to stop falling out by squashing up tight in the watering can's spout.

"Nothing in here!" the little girl said,
and ran off to hunt for more eggs by the shed.

When the egg hunt was over,
the children sat round
and fairly shared out
all the eggs they had found.

Nobody spotted the Tooth Fairy slipping
out of the watering can, tousled and dripping.

She shook out her wings
and then hastily sped
to look for her friend
in the bin by the shed.

Pooh! All she saw was a big heap of yuck –
then up popped the bunny, all covered in muck!

"Humph!" said the bunny. "Oh, fairy, don't grin!
That's the last time I hide in the compost bin!
And you're not much better," he laughed. "What a mess!
You're soaked! Have you been for a swim in your dress?"

The Tooth Fairy smiled and said,

"Fubble-de-fye!"

and as quick
as a flash they
were both
clean and dry.

Then all of a sudden
they heard Gracie shout,
"My wobbly tooth isn't there!
It's come out!"

Poor little Gracie
looked ever so glum.
"If I don't have my tooth,
then the fairy won't come!"

The bunny said,
"Fairy, that isn't true, is it?"
"Oh, no," said the fairy,
"I'll still come and visit.

But I'm sad she's unhappy.
I'll say a quick spell,
we'll find her lost tooth
and then all will be well.

Fibble-di-fubble!
Come here, tooth, to me!

That's strange, it's not working.
Where **can** the tooth be?"

The Tooth Fairy tried out the spell once again –

but the tooth didn't come.

She said, "What a pain!"

The bunny said kindly, "Dear fairy, don't fret.

Just say it once more.

We'll find that tooth yet!"

She tried it again,
and the bunny cried, "Look –
the watering can!
I'm **sure** it just shook!"

They lifted the can up
and instantly found
Gracie's lost tooth,
there on the ground.

The fairy made sure
that the girl didn't see
as she sent off the tooth with a

"Fibble-di-fee!"

Just as the children were going inside
Gracie glanced down at her basket and cried,
"My tooth! Oh, I've found it!" She beamed with delight.
"That means that the Tooth Fairy's coming tonight!"

"I'm so glad she's happy,"
the Tooth Fairy said.
"I'll bring her a coin
when she's tucked up in bed."

"Thank you for all of your help," said the bunny.
"Working with you was exciting and funny.

Now, I still have one egg to deliver," he grinned.
"Bye-bye! I must hurry as fast as the wind!"

The fairy waved "Bye!"
Then she flew home to see . . .

...a shiny bright Easter egg next to her tree!